ORPHAN DREAMER

AND

THE MISSING ARROWHEAD

Episode One
ORPHAN DREAMER SAGA
A Novella: Daniela Rose

A Prequel

J. NELL BROWN

Orphan Dreamer Saga: Episode One
Orphan Dreamer and the Missing Arrowhead: A Novella

Scripture quotations are taken from the Holy Bible, New Living Translation, copyright ©1996, 2004, 2007, 2013, 2015 by Tyndale House Foundation. Used by permission of Tyndale House Publishers, Inc., Carol Stream, Illinois 60188. All rights reserved.

Scripture taken from the New King James Version®. Copyright © 1982 by Thomas Nelson. Used by permission. All rights reserved.

Scriptures taken from the Holy Bible, New International Version®, NIV®. Copyright © 1973, 1978, 1984, 2011 by Biblica, Inc. ™ Used by permission of Zondervan. All rights reserved worldwide. www.zondervan.com The "NIV" and "New International Version" are trademarks registered in the United States Patent and Trademark Office by Biblica, Inc. ™

Published by J. Nell Brown, LLC and Rogue Reads, LLC

"We Wear the Mask"
Words by Paul Laurence Dunbar, 1872-1906
Public Domain

For ordering information, contact the publisher via the author's website, www.JNellBrown.com.

Printed in the United States of America.

First Edition, 2019

Cover by: www.whiterabbitgraphix.com and FrinaArt

ROGUE READS
LLC

BOOKS BY
J. Nell Brown

NONFICTION

Shhh, My Father Is Speaking, and I Am Listening: A Bible Study on Hearing God's Voice

Blood Moon—God's Warning: Why Knowledge of Jewish Feasts Is Essential to Understand the Blood Moons of 2014 and 2015

FICTION

Orphan Dreamer Saga
Orphan Dreamer and the Missing Arrowhead

Orphan Dreamer and the Glass Tattoo

She Laughs Last

Orphan Tree: Rooted in Eternal Love

Collector's First Edition Paperback
The Omega Journey: Blood Moons Whisper

COMING SOON

A Generation of Lighted Evergreens

Orphan Falls: Wild and Free

House Guest

Orphan Star: The Mark

Little Peach Lies

Orphan's Seed

If Love's a Fish

Orphan's Horizon

Orphan's End

Powerful mothers leave a legacy for their children to discover. Purposeful fathers gift their
offspring with a will and a purpose to live. Mine
did. Mom and Dad, thank you.

—J. Nell Brown

and so the
ADVENTURE
begins

Great spirits have always encountered violent
opposition from mediocre minds.

—Albert Einstein

Prologue

One year before . . .
Thursday, April 1, 1993
Gainesville, Florida

EVER SINCE I CAN REMEMBER, I have despised the loneliness, but I never asked for this kind of company.

Not then.

Not now.

Not ever.

It is true: I have begged God for a kindred spirit just like the deliciously independent orphan girl, Anne Shirley, who met and then fell into platonic love with Diana Barry—a beautiful crow-head girl—in Avonlea, the magical lands of *Anne of Green Gables.*

I am not anything to look at, but I am a crow-head. God drenched my curly locks with the same black ink that soaks a crow's wings, and for that bit of goodwill, I am grateful.

But I'm running out of time to find my elusive friend and gift her my homemade friendship bracelet—a chevron pattern of emerald weaved next to black, then plum and lavender, and finally yellow, before starting at emerald again.

Because one night, they will take me in order to save you.

My rafiki—"friend," a.k.a. my dad—told my mom last night. Who knows if I'll be sleeping or awake when they come, but here's hoping that tonight is not that night.

I sweep the butterscotch glow of my flashlight back and forth, searching the cattails by the pond in the middle of my backyard where I ate lunch earlier today. Did I lose the ancient arrowhead here? It's black. An obsidian arrow.

How am I going to find a black arrow in the dirt?

I squint and keep searching. Honestly, I don't remember ever possessing—much less losing—an ancient relic gifted to me by a prince. I'm not exactly the kind of girl a prince would even notice, unless he was the prince of nerds. But I have been a bit confused lately. It's the new medicine. I think.

Suddenly, death warmed over stinks up the sticky air that clings to my skin.

Cattails rustle, whispering a warning. But I haven't found the lost relic yet. I glance over my left shoulder.

Grody. To. The. Max. It's a gator! Heart pounding, I clutch the handle of my quiver. Only one arrow left. It's not ancient. Not special. Not gifted to me by a prince. But this arrow might save my life.

Beneath the yellow sweep of my flashlight, the cold-blooded reptilian belly crawler cursed with a mouthful of jagged and foul-smelling chompers charges out of the pond toward me. I would've been safer in Evergreen Cemetery, lost among moss-laden oak trees, headstones, tombs, and dead people.

Storm!

I bolt across the red wooden bridge that splits the four acres behind our stone cottage in half. Fire shoots up the back of my legs and settles into my calf muscles and thighs. Just two more acres to go. *You can do it, Danny!*

I have to.

Zigzagging, I slosh through a low-lying area of our backyard. Cold mud slings around my ankles, attempting to suck me into the quagmire. I keep pushing forward while focusing on my goal—home, a place of safety.

At least for now.

An amber glow flickers behind the windows of our stone cottage. Mom's probably still up reading. I grit my teeth and propel myself through the ankle-deep sludge. *Should I scream for help? Never. Wimps lose their marbles, then whine about it.* The beast slaps its tail as it snakes its way through the mud, letting me know that it's still on my trail.

One more acre to go.

My lungs scream.

I'm tired.

Time for Plan B.

I launch my body upward, reach up and grab an arm of a moss-draped oak, then scamper up the stairs of the treehouse anchored in the one-hundred-year-old giant's crooked branches.

"Th-th-thanks, Grandpa." Grandpa Cavanaugh died a few years ago, but his legacy—a Swiss Family Robinson fortress—remains. It was a birthday gift to me before he took his last journey to a faraway place. A place where more angels live in the neighborhood than people. In my book, it wouldn't be a bad place to move to. *What do angels look like? I sure could use one about now.*

At the base of the tree, the gator waits for me. Hissing. Snarling. Seemingly shouting that my end lingers closer than I think. But if my end has arrived, then what about Mother and Father?

I need to survive.

For their sakes. Not mine.

I check my pulse. Not dead yet. Mission accomplished.

For a few minutes, I rest while hoping and praying the reptile will grow bored of teasing me, the awkward kid with big hair and a gap-toothed smile. My school bullies usually do. But at almost sundown, the gator must not have anything better to do than add me to his dinner menu. It keeps its beady red eyes trained on me.

Fact one: gators move slower on land than in water.

Stay out of the pond!

Fact two: the vulnerable parts of an alligator are its eyes and its palatal valve.

"Sour milk and mushrooms!" The palatal valve is located at the very back of a gator's throat. The only way I can punch through the palatal valve is if the gator opens its mouth and I stick my arm inside it. Note to self: don't let this situation get to the hand-in-mouth stage. It's what we call a major fail.

And don't get caught in a death roll either. That's an epic fail.

My pounding heart knocks up against my breastbone, sounding just like our rickety screen door on a stormy day.

"Here goes nothing." I reach into my quiver, retrieve my last arrow—tipped with a blunt wooden arrowhead—then load the practically useless weapon into my bow. *Do I try to kill the gator? Especially after the butterfly? That would be a double murder in one day.*

At the age of twelve, has my life deteriorated into this—the life of an assassin? It sounds exhilarating and powerful—killing things—but murder is never really the act of bravery. I grip the rise of my bow, pull the string back, and fire.

Bullseye!

The arrow thumps the gator in the left eye. It rears back its ugly head, bellows, then charges past the oak tree.

With the beast out of sight, I scamper down the tree-house stairs and keep running until I climb up our back-porch stairs, open the screen door, and dive onto the dining room floor. The rickety door cannot close fast enough.

What a fine kettle of a mess I've found myself in, looking in the near dark for an ancient arrowhead that I don't remember having or losing and then getting chased by a gator—as though the reptile was telling me, "Girl, get your behind home. Your momma's waiting for you."

Maybe the inquisitor is right—I'm not all there. I shrug. Maybe I don't want to be there anyway.

Since the obsidian arrowhead supposedly belonged to a prince, my finding it could gain me entry into Claire Anne Underwood's Untouchables.

It's almost seven o'clock, past my bedtime, and it's a school night. I take off my muddy tennis shoes and hide them by the back door of the dining room before I sneak through the kitchen and the living room, then finally arrive to my bedroom. Still feeling breathless, I slip on my pajamas. A bath will have to wait.

My parents cannot know what I was up to.

I wasn't supposed to be eavesdropping last night.

It's true: I'm a swamp girl. I live on the fringes of a swamp. A place where water moccasins, rattlers, and gators hide within cattails. But technically, I live three miles from The Swamp. A field where the Gators—the orange-and-blue variety—dress out in their University of Florida football jerseys before running into The Swamp to fight Georgia's Bulldogs, Florida State University's Seminoles, or Alabama's Crimson Tide.

Us Gators, we're used to sitting at the top of the food chain, just like our namesake, the alligator—an apex predator, according to my science teacher—so our football team and other athletic teams at Florida's oldest university try their best to keep our town riding on top of the coveted tidal wave of the Southeastern Conference.

Or so my rafiki says.

He loves sports. I'm only a lukewarm fan; it's something for a girl to do with her dad on a Saturday afternoon.

One day, when I grow up, I am going to attend college at the University of Florida, where I'll study something scientific like physics, biology, nutrition, chemistry, or mathematics as an undergraduate student. Then I'll apply and matriculate into the College of Medicine.

That's my ten-year plan—to become a medical doctor

and take care of sick children. That is, if I survive 7112 S.E. 221st Avenue—my parents' loving but dangerous lair, a house of secrets. Secrets that, according to my parents, matter for everyone's survival.

Alligators.

Secrets.

An arrowhead that I supposedly lost.

Of course I can't sleep.

I'm bugg'n out. Not because of the swamp, snakes, bugs, or gators. I'm used to those creatures. Have arrows, will travel. But I'm not even thirteen years old, and my Cinderella daydreams have already vanished—only to be resurrected into mutated Frankenstein nightmares.

According to my parents' conversation last night, my destiny has been decided. Plain and simple.

The blueprint of my future doesn't even include the one thing that I have begged for—one solitary friendship bracelet.

I am not picky. The girl who gifts me my very first friendship bracelet doesn't even have to be Claire, the most popular girl in my middle-school class. I know that I'm not good enough to join the Untouchables; but as I said, that ancient arrowhead could give me a fighting chance.

But do I really want to join the Untouchables?

All I ever wanted was my very own *Anne of Green Gables* best friend—a kindred spirit, someone who likes me just as I am.

Tonight, my dream of finding my kindred spirit must be hidden a universe away, rocketed into outer space faster than I depleted my bank of clever circa-1980's slang words. Words that I learned by listening to Claire.

Blonde.

Tall.

Skinny.

But a lightweight in the brain department. Chad Prevington doesn't seem to care if Claire isn't smart though. He thinks she's cool, pretty, and fun. Maybe boys don't like smart girls. Mom and Dad call me precocious, even genius. That's my main problem. Who wants to talk to a precocious genius? It sounds worse than a period—not the punctuation type of period.

Doesn't matter. I'm only twelve, and I'm not allowed to look at boys or even acknowledge their existence—except for Ethan. I press my shoulders into my mattress and jut my chin into the air. But getting to know Ethan was an exception. He's wheelchair bound, so my rafiki felt sorry for him.

I especially cannot talk to boys who look like Chad—rich, pale, and blessed with a Hollywood smile.

So my rafiki says.

I sigh.

I wouldn't know what to do on a date anyway, but all my fourteen-year-old classmates have gone on at least one. Even coke-bottle-glasses Sherry Sanders. That makes me a total dud—a rocket with no fuel to launch.

But could I try to be more like Claire? No. It'd be too hard; she's fourteen years old, perky, and cool. It's easier to talk like myself—a twelve-year-old nerd. I tuck a grin behind my gap-toothed smile because I've got bigger problems.

One day, they will take me. Not Chad or Claire, but someone else. Someone graveyard scary. Worse than an alligator's underwater death roll. And I cannot swim.

When?

How?

Why will they take me?

I don't have a clue. Or at least, I don't know the real reason—the unfiltered, unparented, PG-13 *Raiders of the Lost Ark* version. Last night, I overheard my rafiki talking to my mom. Something about me becoming the next Indiana Jones. That's a joke. I am so not brave. Definitely not swashbuckling-Harrison-Ford brave. Besides, I'm just a girl. Small. Awkward. Brown.

Mom and Dad had whispered something about an ancient puzzle and finding a mysterious key to unlock it. I am good at solving riddles and finding lost things. Ask my mom. When she loses her keys in the morning, I'm her go-to kid. Actually, I'm the only kid.

The key supposedly allows me to conquer an invisible planet called Wormwood.

I understand.

Really, I do.

Every parent wants their kid to grow up and become a hero. The Andersons brag about their son to my parents all the time. Bobby's doing this. Bobby's doing that. My mom and my dad say nothing. But I don't fight, much less conquer planets named after invertebrate animals invading a piece of wood. Who names a planet Wormwood?

Creepy.

Pluto may be small and losing its planet status, but the name Pluto at least sounds planetary.

Last night when my parents had cuddled together on the living room couch, sipping lemonade and talking into the night, I stood hidden in the hallway. Dad had whispered to my Mom, "Chi Xi Stigma." What the heck? Then he talked about taking me on an archeology dig to look for the lost Ark. At best, dirt and I maintain a love-hate relationship. I can be a tomboy, but only when I need to be.

For instance, when running from alligators.

But my parents lost me when they were talking about my traveling to exotic worlds of the past and future. Don't know how I'm going to travel to other worlds, much less afford anything exotic. Dad earns seventeen thousand dollars a year. I saw his tax return. Mom studied at Spelman College to become a teacher but chose to stay home with me until I'm grown up. My allowance consists of five dollars a week. Okay. We're poor, but I'm okay with that because we won't always be poor. Promise.

My rafiki had said something about math problems. At least I rock at math.

But he also had mentioned a pandemic. Disease makes me nervous and itchy all over. My parents call my dislike of viruses, parasites, and bacteria OCD.

OCD. Obsessive Compulsive Disorder—or any other acronym that forms a speed bump in my path to becoming a medical doctor—prepare to be flattened.

Then there was the vilest part: the part about the orphan.

Okay.

Maybe I am a bit sheltered, even naïve.

Can I share a secret?

I have never met or even seen an orphan, at least not while awake. The idea of meeting something or someone who was given away—a kid who didn't and doesn't belong to anyone—scares me to the bone. Because if someone doesn't belong, they don't have anything to lose.

Right?

Maybe I'm also a bit jaded.

Mom explained to me that *jaded* means overly negative; the word jaded reminds me of turquoise-tinted diamonds, so I use the word at every opportunity that arises.

My dad swears that the men in prison commit crimes because they have nothing to lose. No love. No family. No hopes or dreams. Nothing.

I toss and turn, hoping for sleep, but it evades me. If I meet an orphan, will they infect me with their I-don't-want-you-anymore disease? The kids at my school already exclude me. No matter what my parents predict for me, one day I will find my very own *Anne of Green Gables* kindred spirit. Red hair, freckles, and all.

I try to swallow, but my mouth turns cotton dry. Will I become an orphan if I befriend one? Could an orphan's misfortune rub off on me, making my parents die or choose to give me away?

Clenching Grandma's quilt, I bolt up in bed.

They call him—the eyeless boy who has been turning my dreams into nightmares for the last six months—the Orphan.

Not an orphan, but *the* Orphan. As if he is the only one. Sort of like the University of Florida Gators are called The Gators, not *a gator.*

During their not-so-secret conversation, Mom and Dad had called me the Orphan Dreamer. My slight frame quivers more violently than the 1960's Valdivia earthquake that I learned about in Ms. Bender's science class.

I chew the inside of my lip while I remember the quake caused by the Nazca Plate gyrating and grooving across the

South American Plate to the tune of 9.6 on the moment magnitude scale, a.k.a. the new Richter scale. It danced atop the rocky floor of the submarine Peru–Chile Trench in the eastern Pacific Ocean that reaches a maximum depth of 26,460 feet below sea level.

A place of dark, cold, and suffocating death.

I lie back down and dig my toes into the mattress, trying to anchor my body, but I keep shaking. I pull my grandma's patchwork quilt up over my chilled, sweat-drenched body.

Someone opens my bedroom door. My heart skips a beat. My rafiki enters my bedroom, holding a jar in his hand. Shriveled-up yellow wings cling to the bottom of the glass tomb.

He found it.

Warmth fills the back of my nose, then slips down my throat. The hot liquid tastes like nails. "I-I-I didn't mean to kill it, Rafiki. Honest I didn't!" I sniffle hard and swallow a mixture of blood and slimy mucus.

"I believe you, darling." I take a deep breath. My rafiki gives me his handkerchief, then chuckles. "You're a gentle soul. A bit absentminded at times, but you wouldn't—no, you couldn't—swat a bumblebee even if it stung you. But why did you do it, Danny-girl?" He sits on the chair beside my bed.

"I had to help . . . I just had to, Daddy." My voice falls to a whisper. "Sunflower-yellow wings. Miniature black eyes. Dainty feet. She is . . . I mean was . . . so b-b-beautiful." My face flushes. I hate stuttering. So unladylike. Claire would never stutter. She'd refuse to speak, but she'd never stutter.

"God rest its little soul."

I sniffle again. "It's not fair. Buried alive. Suffocating. Being forced to begin as a slimy green worm and then hide its ugliness inside a cramped and dark cocoon. The apricot sulfur didn't deserve to struggle anymore. In my opinion—"

"What's your opinion, my little truth-seeker?"

"The being buried alive part is quite enough misfortune for such an exquisite creature. Don't you agree?" I dab my nose with his handkerchief.

"But by helping the insect, you crippled it."

"I know, and I'm sorry. Devastated, actually. Promise I am. Cross my heart, hope to die."

"I hope you live! Our lives depend upon your staying alive, Danny Rose."

"Really, Dad. It's not right to make up such stories. I'm not special."

"You are special." Daddy smiles wide. "But beauty and life without strength—without suffering—can be a crippling, or even fatal, flaw. Ask Claire. She should know."

Instinct tells me to laugh at my dad's joke but looking at the dead insect stifles any humor inside me. "I'm not beautiful. If that's what you're saying." I divert my gaze away from my dad's kind eyes.

"But you are, and the struggle, baby girl, strengthens the part of the insect that allows it to fly." My dad's voice cracks. "Robbed of its strong wings, it died. Remember this lesson, Danny Rose."

"I will—promise, pinky-swear." My dad links his chunky fifth finger with mine, crushing my twelve-year-old pinky like an anaconda suffocates its prey. He smiles at me, and initially, warmth consumes my shivering frame, but I know the truth: I killed that apricot sulfur—innocent, beautiful, and packed full of sunflower-yellow hope. Cold dread consumes my mind.

Even my rafiki agrees with the verdict: I am a murderer. My heart plummets, sinking thirty thousand feet into the dark-blue depths of the Peru–Chile Trench.

A bone-crushing depth.

Flat-as-a-pancake squished.

Dad's right.

I should feel sadness, because a kid who kills helpless things by crippling their wings no longer deserves empathy from anyone. Guilt and darkness consume me. I face my newest reality. I am no longer daddy's little innocent girl— I am an impatient murderess, a convict just like the men locked behind bars at Florida State Prison, where my dad serves as assistant chaplain. But unlike the inmates, I don't have an excuse. I belong to Austin and Jeanette Cavanaugh, my loving parents.

The apricot sulfur was my first victim.

Dear God, let it be my last!

I deserve a death sentence, but maybe I can make up for my fatal mistake?

"Rafiki." Clenching my bedspread, my nail beds blanch tombstone white. "How much time do we have left?"

"Lord willing and the creek don't rise, enough time for you to change our fate. If you choose to accept your destiny, that is."

"Maybe I will," I whisper.

"Look out, Harrison Ford, there's a new Indiana Jones in town!" Dad laughed.

"Not funny. Fate," I whisper, then sigh. "Definitely not my long-lost kindred spirit."

"Don't be ugly, Danny Rose."

But I am ugly. My face. My skin. My attitude. My future. Horned-lizard ugly.

Beyond my window, two hundred billion stars form a posse and chase the sun's warmth and light out of town. Matching the turmoil churning inside my mind, darkness the color of black ink seeps across the once happy pale-blue sky.

But as always, the sun whispers over its shoulder, "Goodnight, Danny Rose," swipes a kiss with painted lips of golden lavender across Earth's horizon, then skitters down the backside of the western sky—out of sight and out of mind, leaving a swath of shadows and darkness for those eager to get on with their diabolical plans.

It's my least favorite time of day.

Nightfall.

"Don't let them take me, Daddy. Not yet. Please." My lower lip trembles. "Make them wait at least until after my birthday. Even if all my classmates refuse to come to my party, let me stay normal until then."

"Why?" He sits beside me on the bed.

"Because maybe I'll open a big box"—I stretch my arms wide—"that's been tied shut with red ribbon and royal-blue wrapping paper." I wipe a big fat tear from my right cheek and grin, my cheeks quivering. "And maybe . . ." I whisper, "I'll finally find my very own Anne Shirley, my kindred spirit straight out of *Anne of Green Gables*—a girl with matchstick-red hair who chooses to be my friend in spite of my nosebleeds, big hair, and brown skin. Okay, Rafiki?"

"It's not my choice." Dad sniffles and rubs my arm with his calloused thumb. "Never has been, Danny-girl." He folds the handkerchief soaked with my blood, hiding the evidence of my fierce nosebleed. For the third time today, my face flushes volcanic hot.

He kisses my forehead, then clicks off my lamp. The nightlight clicks on. "After you become a big girl, you'll be asked to decipher when, who, what, where, how, and why."

"Then I'll stay small—invisible."

"Not possible." He tucks me beneath grandmother's quilt. "You're our Orphan Dreamer. So dream, my darling one. Spread your wings. Fly. And if the good Lord has a kindred spirit tucked away for you, she will be the lucky one." He winks. No longer daddy's little girl, I am abandoned in the dark as he shuts the door behind him.

I click on my flashlight and study my rafiki's newest word search puzzle, which he made especially for me. The title reads *Your mission, should you accept it: solve the riddle. Find the words that will remind you of your destiny:* WHEN, WHO, WHY, HOW, WHAT, WHERE.

S	V	W	O	S	Y	Y
R	E	H	O	B	H	A
L	W	E	N	H	W	M
O	O	R	B	W	G	I
F	N	E	H	B	V	D
R	G	E	P	B	H	I
Q	N	T	A	H	W	L

I solve the puzzle in ten seconds flat!

Dear Abba Father,

It's me, again.

Sorry to bug you, but if I am the last Orphan Dreamer, how do I become "unchosen" without hurting anyone's feelings?

I want to help, but my schedule's full.

I'm still searching for my kindred spirit, the friend who allows me to be myself, keeps my secrets safe, and helps me punish the two meanest girls at Milweekee Middle School—Claire Underwood and Tameka Jenkins.

If You need another Orphan Dreamer, may I suggest three adults who kick butts and take names every day? Ms. Bender, my science teacher, is smart. FYI: her rambunctious kids will need babysitters. Mrs. Johnson, my school bus driver, is punctual. She smokes. Kicking butt and wheezing may not go together, though.

What about Mom?

She's perfect: wise, beautiful, patient, and a crack shot with a sling and stone! Mom could thump the planet robber on the forehead and knock him out cold.

FYI: fighting Lucifer isn't really a task for twelve-year-olds. Please consider increasing the minimum age for the job. You'd find more willing applicants.

Good night!

Yours truly,

Me, the retired Orphan Dreamer

P.S. If I qualify for hazard pay after serving as Orphan Dreamer for twelve hours, one minute, and two seconds, please send the funds to Dad and Mom. They could use the money for Dad's hospital visits. Thanks.

One snowflake falls from heaven to quench
hell's thirst . . .

1—Orphan Dreamer

Monday, July 11, 1994
Gainesville, Florida

I KILLED HIM.

After my thirteenth birthday, I murdered my best friend—my *only* friend—Ethan.

We should have stayed in Gibeah, but I insisted we return to Milweekee Middle School, a prison whose inmates dressed in Keds tennis shoes and OshKosh jeans. Armed with acne, attitude, and squeaky prepubescent voices, my classmates lived to torture Ethan—the one-legged cripple—and me, his nosebleeding friend with the bushy hair.

"By helping him die, you saved Ethan," my parents told me. Don't worry. Mr. and Mrs. Cavanaugh of 7112 S.E. 221st

Avenue are not sociopaths; they are as normal as parents are allowed to be. Their sympathetic words soothed me, stopping their only child—me—from killing herself too.

Depression sucks.

It's heavy.

Like swimming against riptides your whole life. Still, murdering my only friend—not to mention living to tell the tale—sucks even more.

Depression: a genetic predisposition where happy hormones cannot reach the brain's happiness center, leaving a person without the ability to experience pleasure and appropriately deal with trauma.

—J. Nell Brown

2—Orphan Dreamer

1st of Tishri 1018 B.G.E.
Yom Teruah (Rosh Hashanah)
Gibeah

FOR THOUSANDS OF YEARS, THE Glass Tattoo waited.

On a moonless, starry night—as I stand beside Ethan's bed, watching him die—the relic abducts the Orphan Dreamer. Me. I arrive in Gibeah as an orphan. We both do. Nameless and alone, save for each other and our masters. Dew kisses my mahogany cheeks; I open my eyes. Chains clank around my feet. Nearby, a whip cracks, followed by a scream. My throat dries. "I'm scared."

"Don't be. This place is magical. Look." My friend points to his right leg, and I gasp.

"It grew back."

"Back in the game for the last inning." His eyes twinkle. Nearby, a man drags a child away from his mother.

"Don't let them separate us." I squeeze Ethan's hand.

"Over my dead body."

As the sun peeks above a horizon of craggy hills, Prince Jonathan, heir to the Hebrew throne, purchases us from a slaver's caravan. The prince names his thirteen-year-old slaves Shiloh and Ezra, stripping us of our former identities and places in the world.

Shackles released, I clutch my tattered bag as we trek across the Sahara.

Sunrise bleeds the night of stars, igniting the heavens with flames the colors of a bruised tangerine. Ezra and I shiver beneath the fiery sky, the sun refusing to share its warmth until it peaks in the midday sky. Rays of hope nourish our slight frames, clothed in threadbare tunics and turbans.

Hot sand burns my bare feet, and the stench of camels irritates my nose.

Slavery sucks!

Ezra—gifted with brand-new, fast legs—runs ahead, not caring about his invisible chains of slavery because in Gibeah he can run.

Behind me, horses' hooves pound across the Sahara. Beasts snort and neigh, the earth shaking beneath their stampede.

I dodge right.

"Walk decisively, young man!" My posture snaps straight. To my left, a burly man dismounts his black stallion. "Your name, child?"

"Da-Da-Da . . . I-I-I mean, the prince calls me Shiloh."

"Names." A smirk pushes a jagged scar away from the big man's nose. "Deceptive realities."

"Sir?"

"The prince calls me General of the Guard—Jehu—but I am no eager assassin." He hardens his square jawline. "I am a father. A widow. A simple man who life has forced to master the sword." He rests his hand on my head. "We are greater than our names."

He's crazy! I'm nobody, a slave.

"These are perilous times, child."

No kidding. Yesterday, I was standing beside Ethan's deathbed. Now, I'm a slave forced on a dust march to nowhere.

"The Philistines have declared war." The general lifts my chin with his finger. "The world requires heroes, not victims." Masculine sweat and fermented breath fill my nose.

"I-I-I'm not a victim. Mom says."

"Good. Victims are defeated in their thoughts, first and foremost."

"I'm not your hero, either."

"Heroes don't know who they are until the mission calls." He releases my chin. "At week's end, I'll be recruiting young lads, training them to be warriors. Come. Train."

"I'm no fighter, either." My eyes burn with fear.

"Then what are you?" Disdain poisons his tone.

"A kid . . . who misses home." I try to swallow.

"My Miriam misses her dead mother, yet still, she wishes to fight—but she's a girl, and in Gibeah, that is her curse. No girls in the prince's army." He smiles wryly. "But you're a boy. You can fight." He balls up his fists. A flutter dances in my stomach. Even generals can be wrong, but with fists like those . . .

"I'm a peacemaker, not a fighter."

"Peace eludes those unwilling to fight for it." He pulls his stallion's reigns; the beast canters alongside us. "Let me tell you a secret, child."

"I like secrets." Friends share their secrets. Miriam's father chortles. "A hero's journey rarely begins in fancy places. It starts in the lowest places. In solitude. In obscurity. Where a boy's character hardens into the iron will of a man."

"But Claire's popular . . . never mind."

"I don't know Claire, but after our four hundred and thirty years of Egyptian slavery, the God of Israel remembered us and delivered us from that obscurity with an outstretched hand. He will do it again."

"I know." I smile, remembering Apostle Matthew's account of Yeshua's birth. "The Messiah was born over two thousand years ago in a Bethlehem stable, because there was no room for Him to be born in an inn."

"You're mistaken," Miriam's father says. I furrow my brow. He continues, "The God of Israel will seek out warriors to defeat our enemies. Be ready for war!"

Miriam's dad is wrong.

Yeshua—the Messiah—has come, not as a warring king but as the prophet Isaiah's sacrificial lamb who paid for humanity's wrongs. But in Gibeah, the general reigns as master. *Would he punish a disagreeable slave?*

Another braided rawhide whip snakes across the back of a slave.

"As you wish, General," I say.

But sign up to fight?

Kids know their limits.

Mine: I don't brawl.

Mother wouldn't tolerate it! Even the Messiah says, "Blessed are the peacemakers for they will inherit the Kingdom of God."

"Hear, O Israel, the Lord is our God, the Lord is one," the general cries at the top of his lungs. My ears throb and my heart races as the members of the royal caravan shout a response. "You shall love the Lord, your God, with all your heart, with all your soul, and with all your mind."

"Little one, why love Adonai?" *Disagreeable slaves. Punishments. Best to keep quiet.* I shrug. "Love for Adonai fuels our compassion for His creation—ourselves and our neighbors."

"Love myself?" I laugh. "Claire and Harry hate me."

Miriam's father tilts his chin. "Those are odd names."

"I agree." I grin slyly, loving the fact that Miriam's dad thinks something about my school bullies is odd. Add General Jehu to the short list of possible kindred spirits.

"We are only capable of loving our neighbors to the same degree we love our Creator and ourselves. This is the purpose of your journey to Gibeah. Learn to trust Adonai with everything, including your friend's life." He points at Ezra, who plays with a stray dog. I shiver in the one-hundred-degree weather.

"Sacrifice. It courses through every hero's veins." He refuses to get it. I am not a hero!

"Loving myself . . . not possible. Trust me."

"It is necessary! No one saves someone they loathe." His eyes twinkle, as if he knows my secret. "You're no ordinary child."

Sour milk and mushrooms! He knows. "B-b-but I am ordinary."

"You want to be ordinary. There's a difference." What kid doesn't want to be normal? I push my turban down, covering my ears and almost my eyes. Best to hide my other enigma. In Gibeah, that secret equals a curse.

"You're like my Miriam."

"H-h-how?" My heart pounds beneath my tunic.

"You listen to others' secrets, refusing to share your own."

"Rosh Chodesh! Rosh Chodesh is sanctified!" Two horsemen ride from the eastern mountains toward the western valley.

"What are they saying, General?"

"Look up." He kneels and points toward the cloudless sky. "The priests' watchmen are proclaiming that a new moon has been sighted." A silver crescent moon cuts a sliver out of the sky. "We call the new moon the *twinkling of an eye.*"

"Why?" I whisper.

"Because the crescent looks like a partially opened eyelid, and this new moon is special, signaling the beginning of the ecclesiastical year, the day Adonai created the heavens and the earth. But most importantly, the new moon signals the beginning of the month Tishri, which signifies the start of our fall feasts."

"I know. The feast with shofar blasts, then a Day of Atonement, followed by the feast of dwelling in booths."

"How did you know?"

"Mom told me."

"Wise woman." He pats my head. "These are happy times. We celebrate wonderful themes during the fall feasts:

repentance, kingship, coronation, and marriage. And Moses received the second set of tablets—the marriage contract between Elohim and Israel—in Tishri."

"Cool," I say. The general furrows his brow and looks at me, then laughs. *A Hebrew Cinderella story.* I grin, liking the idea that one day a king would come looking for his bride. "Mom says that in our land, some people celebrate themes of resurrection during Tishri."

"Why?" the general cocks his head.

"Don't know." I shrug. "Never asked. Tell me more about your customs."

"The watchmen guide their steeds across the hillside as fast as lightning bolts from east to west, lighting bonfires."

"Is the direction of the lightning important?"

"The direction answers the riddle. Lightning comes out of the East and shines to the West, just as the Tribe of Judah camped on the eastern side of the Tabernacle and the Holy of Holies rested on the western side."

"So will the coming of the Messiah be. 'I tell you a mystery. We will not all sleep, but we will all be changed, in a moment, in the twinkling of an eye.'" I recite the Apostle Paul's riddle given to the Corinthian believers. I gaze at the twinkle of the new moon. "My first clue."

"You are confusing when you want to be." General Jehu mounts his stallion, looks down at me, and smiles. "But what girl isn't?"

"Girl!" I stumble backward.

"It'll be our secret. Tuck those wayward locks beneath your turban." He grabs a tuft of the stallion's mane. "Keep your friends and secrets close. One day, Melech Melechai Melechim—the King of all Kings—will come looking for you—a slave girl destined to become His hero."

"I don't want to fight." My face flushes volcanic hot. "I'll run away!"

"And be swallowed by a giant fish."

Does he mean Jonah, the Hebrew prophet?

But . . . how did the general know this story? Jonah wouldn't be born for another two hundred or so years.

Jonah is the one who refused to warn the Ninevites about Yahweh's impending judgment. Running away from his calling, Jonah boarded a ship only to be tossed into the ocean after a storm almost capsized the vessel. A big fish swallowed the drowning prophet, keeping him safe. After three days, he surrendered to Yahweh's call, and the fish spit him onto dry land.

Jonah warned the Ninevites.

They repented and were saved from judgment.

"The ones you love will suffer if you keep running." The general's voice pulls me back to the present. He rides into the horizon, his horse kicking sand into my face.

I cough while pondering his words. Ezra is still running and teasing the desert creatures.

Isn't he exhausted?

I am.

In the quiet of my soul, I breathe four wishes: to reclaim my identity, see my parents again, never lose Ethan, and follow Yeshua until time overtakes me, propelling me into my Messiah's arms for forever. Some call that last part death, but I'm trying to think positive. In exchange for my freedom, the inquisitor demands this of me.

Though frail, my hope will be hard to kill.

But what about the Glass Tattoo?

I open my fist, shivering at the sight of the translucent snowflake that buried itself inside my right palm last night before darkening into a midnight-blue tattoo.

The tattoo has marked me, ordering me to become someone I don't believe I can become: the Orphan Dreamer, a warrior destined to wield the God factor, a powerful weapon designed to set captives free. The Glass Tattoo demands all. My past. My present. My future. And even the sweet calm of my dreams.

Suddenly, the animals disappear from the desert. Prince Jonathan, Ezra, and the rest of the caravan vanish.

I'm alone!

"Wake up," I scream, hoping to escape this desert nightmare.

As if the same dark force overheard my cry—the same one Father warned would annihilate humans and claim the world—Earth's enemy summons the sand dragon, and the entire surface of the desert rises in obedience. A fiery sandstorm blacks out the sky. Tiny soldiers made of grain hurtle toward me.

Hope bleeds from my veins as the dragon's fiery chariots surround me. His breath scorches my face, striking my legs with rocks until blood runs.

Fight or retreat?

I search for a weapon but find none. I cower and roll into a ball. The sand dragon thrashes me until he almost breaks me. "I'm alone. I can't do this." My body and soul throb. "Help."

An answer arrives in the form of a question: What element quenches fire? Mom's biblical sayings guide me: ". . . washed by water and the cleansing of God's Word."

Water is my weapon. The dragon's mortal enemy.

I rise.

The sandstorm ebbs.

Bruises splotch my skin.

Pain pulses through my muscles. Still, while falling more than walking, I scour the desert until I find its treasure—an oasis. A deep pool ripples beneath a canopy of date palms.

I can't swim.

Breathing with purpose, I consider my options: remain on dry land and certainly die—or attempt to swim and possibly die. Sand sticks to the insides of my nose, ripping open delicate blood vessels. My nose bleeds.

Squeezing my nostrils, I wade into the pool.

Tepid water tickles my feet, then laps around my thighs. Water encircles my neck. The general's prophetic words mock me: "Sacrifice runs through every hero's veins."

Sacrifice.

How does it feel?

Like unfiltered anguish. *My God! My God! Why have You forsaken me?* The words of the suffering Messiah as He took His last breath while hanging from a Roman cross ring true. But for Mom, Dad, and Ethan, I take a deep breath and dive deep.

Dark waters spill over me, and I pray—no, beg: *Yeshua, swim with me.* After holding my breath for several seconds, I inhale.

Water burns my lungs as though the smooth liquid were hell's fuel—fire.

\#IamDaniela . . .

Flight of Ideas: a rapid shifting of ideas with only superficial associative connections between them that is expressed as a disconnected rambling from subject to subject and occurs especially in the manic phase of bipolar disorder.

—Merriam Webster Dictionary

3—Orphan Dreamer

ETHAN'S DEAD.

The sky and I are still mourning. Grey clouds weep, spilling fat raindrops on my windows as I stand at the foot of my bed, my hands trembling. My Scooby-Doo night-light flickers, throwing shadows in a dark room.

Don't be a scaredy-cat. Open it.

I open my dresser drawer. My heart stops. *It's gone!* Someone stole Prince Jonathan's arrowhead. I run my sweaty fingers across the divot imprinted into the jewelry box's empty velvet lining.

Don't panic. Think like a sleuth. Did I lose it on the way back? Maybe I imagined its existence. Adrenaline surges through my veins. Hot liquid floods my right nostril.

Not now!

I cup my hand under my nose, catching a gush of blood and choking on the rest as I sop up the mess with a tissue.

Tonight, I officially possess a problem bigger than nosebleeds. Without the ancient arrowhead, my thirteen-year-old problems dwarf even the impending apocalypse.

How can I prove my sanity to the inquisitor?

If he pronounces me insane, I'm gone—locked up, key thrown into the Mariana Trench. Sweat glues my pajamas to my back. No awkward kid could stop the apocalypse laced up in a straitjacket and imprisoned inside a puke-green pediatric mental ward.

You live on Earth.

Any suggestions?

I slip into bed, loathing the idea of being labeled the Orphan Dreamer and then punished for being chosen.

"Wake up," I whisper, but my eyes remain wide open. Rain showers boil over into a thunderstorm. Tree branches lash against my windows. Clouds spit terawatts of violence across the heavens.

It's war.

But who's fighting and why?

4—Nomed

FIVE COSMIC REVOLUTIONS
IMMORTALS—TIME WITHOUT END

ONE BLACK WING, TIPPED WITH metal hooks, pops through, followed by the other, as Nomed pushes himself into the unseen world. Huffing for breath, he catches up to Yahweh's warrior. "I'd like to introduce you to my understudy."

A grotesque humpbacked creature with five legs and cyanotic purplish skin infected with oozing green pustules lumbers toward the two warriors. "Her name is Aglaope. The humans call her depression. She's beautiful, isn't she?"

"Why is she here?"

"To visit the girl, your Orphan Dreamer."

"You'll never kill her."

"Don't intend to. Once depression finishes with Rose, she'll kill herself—then her dreams will perish, slaughtering everyone inside of them, including the Orphan."

"Aglaope's resume isn't flawless."

"You're forgetting the power of the inquisitor. If he convinces Rose's mother to doubt her child's sanity, could the Orphan Dreamer survive a mother's disbelief in her very essence—her reality?" Nomed shrieks a laugh. "No—never. Her hope will be wiped out by her own mother. With hope dead, Rose won't even fight back before she takes her own life. I've perfected the process; it works."

"My charge will refuse to believe your lies."

"I am persuasive. Remember unbelief . . . how many humans believe in—and even love—my gift of money but refuse to believe in Yeshua's sacrificial love for them?"

5—ORPHAN DREAMER

THE INQUISITOR WAITS FOR ME.

This is my punishment for murdering Ethan and harming myself.

My mom takes me in my favorite outfit: a faded-pink corduroy jumper over a white button-up shirt and a pair of hot-pink jelly shoes, fresh off layaway from Pic 'N' Save. This morning, before I climbed into the back seat of Mom's banana boat—a 1969 sunburst-yellow Ford LTD—Papa hugged me and whispered, "A mother's love knows no limits. Remember this."

He hates lying.

From his perspective, he isn't, but I don't think he's right. I sit quietly in the backseat of Mom's car and try to understand his point.

According to him, Mom's pushing me through a dime-sized hole down there not only stretched her wider than a dinner plate but also kneaded her heart muscles into a doughball the size of Jupiter and tougher than Teflon. And somehow that same big, floppy heart overflows with a limitless supply of love—for me?

My science teacher taught me that when you stretch any material, it weakens its tensile strength. So let's just say that my mom's heart, though ginormous, has a hull at least as thin as a milk jug.

"You're stabbing me in the heart, Danny Rose!" Mom said after she caught me for the umpteenth time reading *Anne of Green Gables* instead of doing my homework. Try ramming a knife of disappointment into the bottom of a milk jug.

The milk gushes out.

Duh!

I tried it during one of my ultra-secretive science projects. The ones conducted at night in my private lab—the kitchen—after my overseers (parents) fell asleep. Milk soaked my favorite nightgown, and I slept in it.

Big mistake.

My room stank for a week.

Nope, her overstretched heart can't possibly hold enough love for me—her scrawny, ugly, delusional kid.

Not possible.

Flight of ideas. My ideas are flying again! Catch the butterflies, Danny Rose. I forcefully exhale a breath from my nose. My thoughts slow. But would Papa—my rafiki—lie to me?

Okay, so maybe the proverb "love has no limits" was true up until middle school when Mom's awkward, gap-toothed daughter was accused of having serious emotional problems, including delusional thoughts.

It's a secret. I sort of believed Papa when he told me I was destined to become the next Indiana Jones and that the only difference between me and the swashbuckling Harrison Ford was that I was born with two X chromosomes, nosebleeds, curly hair, knobby knees, an inability to acquire friendship bracelets, and brown skin.

Ugh. Tight, curly hair and brown skin. So misunderstood in America!

Please listen very carefully . . . I will only say this once. *I don't want to become Indiana Jones.*

I want to become *Anne of Green Gables'* Diana Barry—a kindred spirit and a normal, pretty girl who doesn't murder her best friend but listens to her friend's deepest secrets, doesn't tease her, and gives her the benefit of the doubt.

We can even exchange friendship bracelets!

Blinking back disappointment, I rub my right wrist. Unlike Claire—a popular girl with more friends than Bugs Bunny—no friendship bracelets.

That rips, bad.

6—ORPHAN DREAMER

03:58 P.M.
TUESDAY, OCTOBER 11, 1994
GAINESVILLE, FLORIDA

WE PARK THE BANANA BOAT outside the inquisitor's office.

On a seafoam-green bench inside the office, I scoot closer to my mom.

A smile brushes across her delicate features, painting fine lines into her smooth brown skin. Beneath long black lashes, she gazes out the double-paned windows and whispers, "The sun is shining on you, Danny Rose. He's on your side even when you can't see Him through the storm." Her feathery voice calms my tattered spirit. "Don't be afraid, my darling." She interlinks her fingers with mine. "When you were born, do you know what I said?"

"Go back where you came from?" I slump into a wilted-lettuce pose. She laughs. "No, honey-dipped bumblebee."

"Gosh, she's an alien?"

"No." Mom chuckles. "I recited the words of my favorite poem . . . 'Here sleeps a girl with a head full of magical dreams, a heart full of wonder, and hands that will shape the world.' " She presses her hand into the middle of my back, forcing me to sit ballerina straight.

"Thanks, Mom." I look down at my hands. They shake as I clutch what's left of a disintegrated tissue in my right hand, pressing pieces of it to my left nostril to stop another nosebleed. So much for shaping the world.

The office door opens.

The inquisitor enters.

I stare out the much-too-big-for-privacy windows. I don't see what Mother sees, and that's a problem. Instead, gray clouds hang pregnant with black dread, and an ever-present ache throbs deep inside my bones. The inquisitor calls the ache depression. I call it a major pain in the butt. I'm certain the ache is the symptom of a real disease, like Ethan's bone cancer that rotted him from the inside out.

I held his hand the day I killed him.

No one should die alone.

7—ORPHAN DREAMER

TUESDAY, OCTOBER 11, 1994
GAINESVILLE, FLORIDA

"DANIELA ROSE," THE INQUISITOR SAYS.

"Yes, sir. That's me." I rest my hands in my lap.

"Beautiful name."

"Thanks."

"I believe you are suffering from flight of ideas."

"That's not so bad. Butterflies fly. I love butterflies, especially the apricot sulfur."

"You misunderstand." He clears his throat. "You are suffering from schizoaffective disorder, depressive type, and this causes your flight of ideas." An imaginary drumroll begins. "How does that make you feel?"

My back stiffens. *How would that make you feel, smarty-pants? Be polite. Mom's watching.* I gaze at the ceiling.

Stupid.

Unworthy of Claire's friendship bracelets.

A total waste of space. I take a deep breath and swallow the ache, but it explodes into a throb. I grab my chest. *Don't lose your heart; it's where you remember Ethan. Calm down. Just sound smart—no, sound sane!* "Umm . . . I don't know."

Major fail. Red lights seem to flash all around me as alarms sound in my mind.

"Daniela, I'm here to help you."

"Really?" The Spanish Inquisitors never "helped" their victims per se.

"It's what I'm paid to do."

I glance at Mom, and she nods. Maybe he is telling me the truth.

"Depression feels like a semitruck's wheel grinding me into a pile of manure while school bullies laugh at me as I try to wiggle free. But I stay trapped, drowning in plain view. Nowhere to hide."

"Ooookay. Vivid."

Mom dabs her eyes with a tissue, but the inquisitor's expression never changes—flat, unfeeling, just doing his job. "I understand."

"Do you believe me?" I hold my breath.

Mom clears her throat. Nope. Understanding is different than believing.

Although the arrowhead is missing, I possess another ace. In my sweaty left hand, I hold a neatly folded letter— the final defense of my sanity, the key to my freedom, and the ticket to sit next to Ethan's grave and apologize for making him leave Gibeah.

"Your teachers report that you are obsessed with a character from a children's novel called *Anne of Green Gables*. Is this true?"

"Not obsessed, just keenly interested."

"Why?"

"Anne and I understand each other. We both long for kindred spirits."

"Have you met Anne?"

"Not yet, but soon."

"Interesting . . . Define a kindred spirit."

"A friend who holds my heart and stops the bleeding."

"Interesting. Are there any other redheads that you're obsessed with?" He massages his sparse goatee.

"Umm." I finger the edge of the letter hidden beneath my thigh. "No, sir."

"You sure?"

My Dearest Adelaide Rose . . .

I recite the contents of the letter in my head, but none of it makes sense anymore.

My heart thumps hard against my chest as I ponder the possibility that the inquisitor and my classmates are right about me.

Maybe the letter proves nothing, except that I *am* crazy—my mind lost in a black hole of wrong turns, stop signs, and do-not-enters as I search for an elusive ginger who is destined to become my kindred spirit.

Vacate Earth now!

Because if I'm your new Indiana Jones, Earth is so doomed.

8—Orphan Dreamer

My Dearest Adelaide Rose,

My life is a Georges-Pierre Seurat painting—and I'm mortified.

For two years, Seurat tapped his fine-tip brush onto a stretched canvas like a Morse coder, leaving a trail of minuscule yet distinct dots of oil paint that shared his story of an 1884 Parisian *Sunday Afternoon on the Island of La Grande Jatte*. I am that painting, half-done: a mosaic of colorful dots, insignificant on its own and not yet organized enough to count as a masterpiece.

Not at all what I had imagined for my life.

As an awkward and lonely girl, I studied art

history and dreamed my autobiography would resemble a Simmie Knox portrait, layered with fluid and purposeful strokes of color meant to capture the character, spirit, and personality of the subject in a dignified manner.

Instead, my story became Seurat-like, scattered into a million fragments. Even so, I attempted to assemble the details of my life into a logical story line and create my own Simmie Knox portrait of my journey before I died. I failed, leaving you to pick up the pieces.

Truly, I am sorry.

Pity is a road I've refused to travel, even though, according to some, I have every right to pick up a map and find my way onto its path. But I knew that would lead to a dead-end and an even deader soul. So, my dearest Adelaide, do not pity yourself, even though you will soon become an orphan. Celebrate life!

Sail the world with Cordelia.

But before you leave, open your gifts. Your father purchased a gift for me before he disappeared. I gift it to you. Inside the wooden case, hidden beneath layers of shipping paper, you'll find the original study of Seurat's *Sunday Afternoon on the Island of La Grande Jatte*. Initially, I was angry with your father for spending so much money for the masterpiece. I don't mind so much anymore since it's now yours. If destiny is to take a mother and a father from you, then maybe this priceless masterpiece will soothe your heart, reminding you of us.

Your second gift is a quilt, made by my great-grandmother. There was a time when fabric squares hid mysteries, telling an escaped slave how to find a train that would escort them underground to freedom.

Escape before it's too late.

Keep your last gift inside its special case. It is the original score of "Blessed Assurance," my mother's favorite hymn. Harriet Tubman, a conductor on the train of bravery and freedom, understood that a song wasn't all notes, words, and tempo.

A riddle: follow the lead in a rich, soulfully syncopated rhythm in C major. CeCe Winans sang the hymn best when your father and I attended the Cicely Tyson Kennedy Center Honors, where we said hello to the First Family for the last time.

I was never brave enough to tell you, but when I was thirteen, a psychiatrist diagnosed me with depression and childhood schizophrenia. Hence, the flight of ideas. Mother and I refused to believe him. Maybe he was right and we were wrong. But in order to fulfill my destiny—which didn't include collecting friendship bracelets—I needed to believe his diagnosis was more appropriately translated as "You're different, and I don't understand different."

Was I crazy?

Was I a bad mother?

You be my judge, my darling daughter, my Adelaide Rose. You are breathtakingly beautiful, brave, and very sane, so I give you permission to venture into the melancholic chaos of my muddled legacy. Maybe you can create a Simmie Knox portrait out of it after all.

Most of all, finish school, be your own woman, and make a difference.

With all my love,
Mommy, Daniela Rose Cavanaugh

9—ORPHAN DREAMER

THE LETTER MAKES ME SOUND ancient—like an Egyptian mummy. No, more like an adult, stuck in the past and a stickler for being quiet and staying still.

The inquisitor looks me up and down, then sideways, a sneer lurking on the edge of his lips. I shrink back.

Am I that repulsive?

I get it.

Awkward thirteen-year-old girls don't write letters to their perfect, redheaded seventeen-year-old daughters if for no other reason than the math doesn't work. I rock at math, even aced trigonometry this school year.

I shift in my seat. If they find the letter, they'll lock me up for sure. *Storm!*—gotta get out of this prison. My legs tense, but I can't bolt. Running can get a scared kid shot in the back by overeager adults.

After a long pause, he says, "Tell me what I should believe."

"I . . ." my voice drops to the whisper of a falling leaf, "traveled to Gibeah."

His rising eyebrows—bushy, lawnmower required—say hello to his receding hairline. I swallow an ill-timed belly laugh.

"You told me someone gifted you an artifact before you left your imaginary world." Wonder why I call him the inquisitor? Please figure it out as I sit in his courtroom, his accusations flying at me with no jury and no witnesses, except for my emotional mother.

"Prince Jonathan gave me the arrowhead." I chew my upper lip and taste blood.

"A prince gave you a gift?" His emphasis lands on *prince* and *you*. The inquisitor glares at me; his watery eyes could drown a rat. "Where is it?" *Appear calm.* "Someone stole it from my bedroom."

"Oh, I see."

Mom squeezes my hand and doesn't release it. *Uh-oh. I messed up!*

"Ms. Cavanaugh, any break-ins recently?"

"No," she whispers.

"Daniela, why don't you stay with us for a while," the doctor says. And by *us*, he means the mental ward for kids. Every kid needs a vacation—but not this kind. "I want to go home." I look at my mom and squeeze her hand for emphasis. "Please, Mom. Don't leave me here. I won't fit in. I'm not crazy. I-I-I'll make you proud. Promise."

"Doctor, we can take care of her at home. We live on four acres, and fresh air soothes any rumpled soul."

The doctor twirls his pen for a full twenty seconds as though he's reading a crystal ball before determining my fate. "Bring Daniela back in a week. I'll make my final decision then, but keep a close eye, Ms. Cavanaugh. We don't want an incident." He means self-mutilation. And the big 'S', suicide.

I slip the letter over my right forearm, hiding the pale, jagged scar. My classmates' verdict was spot on: Daniela Rose Cavanaugh is a nut.

Eventually, all nuts crack.

Especially when the inquisitor—the nutcracker—sits in front of a trembling nut. Me.

But if I surrender and give up, I die; Mother and Papa die; and everyone else dies, including the inquisitor and the bullies at my school.

Mother and Papa don't deserve death; neither did Ethan.

My bullies?

Maybe Earth would be better off without them.

"What is that?" He points at my secret letter. "Nothing." I swallow my fear and set out on a brave journey: face the inquisitor. I blink and then lock eyes with him. He scoots back in his chair. Stutters. Shifts in his seat.

I'm fighting back. He knows.

It's my turn to smile—tight-lipped, bashful, a small hidden victory. My head lifts just above the black pit named depression, and a splash of sunlight bathes my face. The Son. Maybe He is on my side after all.

Hope.

That's all I need. One more day, one more step, and in time, I will climb out of this depressive abyss, then fly away like an apricot sulphur escaping its dark cocoon.

I am Daniela Rose.

And I am powerful.

10—Orphan Dreamer

"FORGIVE YOURSELF." MOM HOLDS MY hand as we escape the inquisitor's frigid lair into a sticky, summer evening. My heart worms its way into my throat.

"I can't."

"Ethan's death wasn't your fault."

"Mom-sympathy votes don't count. I'd do anything to bring him back. Even embrace slavery in Gibeah."

"What? We don't embrace slavery for anyone . . . your ancestors are rolling in their grave."

"Loneliness is its own form of slavery. They would understand." Silence hangs thick between us. "Mom . . ."

"Yes, bumblebee?"

"Do you believe me?"

She waits to answer. "If you could remember where you left the arrowhead, the doctor could believe you." Disbelief shines through her eyes.

"I traveled to Gibeah."

"I'm not saying—"

"You'll see, Mom. You'll see I'm not crazy." Before I yank my hand out of hers and race to the banana boat, I scream, "I'm done telling my story. No one listens. Adelaide will tell it. People will believe her. She's a ginger."

"Who's Adelaide?"

I ignore Mom's question.

No need to appear certifiably insane on this bright summer day. The ability to perceive reality—truth—from fiction should never be taken for granted, but who defines truth?

A prism bends light, and according to Dad, historians and politicians bend the truth into accepted facts. A dictator bends his subject's will.

I bend time, distorting my reality—and maybe yours.

The shrink calls my gift schizophrenia.

My questions: Is Yahweh a comedian? If not, why rely upon a depressive schizo to save the world? Because maybe in His reality, I am *not* insane. And just maybe the fight requires a person most humans cannot figure out—a girl crazy enough to believe in kindred spirits, fight Lucifer, and win.

One day, I'll find the arrowhead. Prove my sanity. And maybe even kick Lucifer's butt.

In the meantime, trust me. What do you have to lose—everything?

Me too.

Reality is merely an illusion, albeit a very persistent one . . .

—Albert Einstein

Facts are created, but Truth bears a name—Yeshua says, "I am the way and the truth and the life. No one comes to the Father except through me" (John 14:6 NIV).

11—Adelaide: #Mom. It's Greek to Me

I'M CHEWING THE LAST OF my fingernails down to the nub as I sit at a reading carrel inside Phillips Exeter's Library, hunched over a closed calculus textbook, a three-ring binder, and Mother's weathered journal.

I stole the journal.

I needed to.

The last few bars of Steven Curtis Chapman's "I Will be Here"—one of my da's favorite ballads to chisel away at Mother's crumbling wall of nos before you know what—plays through my earbuds as I stare at the carrel's back panel, letting the bass notes vibrate the strings of my soul.

What can I say?

They are crazy about each other, but their craziness didn't conceive me, and for now, that's my secret. My bestie, Cordy Grey, doesn't even know. Thinking about my parents' tenacious love, I relish a quick smile, then glance over my shoulder.

No spies.

Gingerly, I open Mother's journal and stare at the first page.

Pages crinkle, eager to tell me their secrets.

As though an invisible force wants me to snoop on my own mother, a folded sheet of lilac-scented paper falls into my lap. I retrieve the insert and attempt to decipher her doctor's handwriting:

> Legend says Yeshua's last surviving apostle, John, penned a riddle before he died on the Isles of Patmos. The riddle's answer possesses the power to save humanity from annihilation by a future tyrant.
>
> *Hode este sophia* means "here is the riddle."
>
> "Here is the riddle. Let him that hath understanding count the number of the beast: for it is the number of a man; and his number is Six hundred threescore and six—Chi Xi Stigma" (Revelation 13:18).

I stare at the three random Greek letters, desperate for answers. "Chi Xi Stigma . . ." I repeat that several times before it clicks.

"In the language of mathematics," I whisper. "Chi Xi Stigma is a palindrome, like *racecar* or *taco cat*—spell it backwards and it says the same thing. But this is better than a typical palindrome since it's a number."

Mathematics is universal. *Sweet pickle juice!*

I find a blank page in my three-ring binder while trying to conjure up the fading details of my Greek language lessons.

Slowly, I jot down my answer: *Chi, Xi, and Stigma are Greek letters with the gematria of 600, 60, and 6.*

Chi=600. Xi=60. Stigma=6.

But do I add the numbers together—666—or interpret them separately? I continue reading her note.

> Adonai gave His prophet Daniel a vision, and Daniel penned these words: "But as for you, Daniel, conceal these words and seal up the scroll until the end of time" (Daniel 12:4).
>
> Adelaide, the key to solving the mystery of the scroll and unlocking the riddle is wisdom.
>
> What is wisdom?
>
> Judea's wisest leader—King Solomon—wrote, "The fear of the Lord is the beginning of wisdom" (Proverbs 9:10). The Hebrew word for *fear* translates into the modern English word *reverence*—not terror. Adelaide, you must enter

into a close relationship with Yahweh in order
to learn His secrets and solve this final riddle.

With all my love,
Mommy

P.S. Hint: wisdom is not a "thing."

She is a person: "I, wisdom, was with Adonai when He began His work, long before He
made anything else. I was created in the very
beginning, even before the world began. I was
born before there were oceans, or springs over-
flowing with water . . ." (Proverbs 8:22-24).

Take the time to meet her one day!

Footsteps thud on the carpet, nearing my desk. Quickly, I
fold the letter and stuff it into my backpack alongside Mother's letter about Seurat paintings. The footsteps pass, leaving
me to remember.

A soft-spoken North Carolina minister once said, "The
sins of the fathers are visited upon their children's heads
to the third and fourth generations." Mother, Father, and I
were the only people in attendance that Sunday, so I kind of
believe the message was for us.

But what if a kid's parents were perfect, like mine?

I smile—tight-lipped, knowing I'm blowing smoke. No
parents are perfect, but let's say that mine are. Then, according to that North Carolina preacher, my seventeen-year-old,
rich-girl life should flow smoother than Oregon's glacier-fed

Crater Lake; or at least, this is my perception of the Guy Upstairs's rules.

No ripples.

Definitely no waves.

Right?

Wrong.

Because as of late, my day-to-day is akin to a Category 5 hurricane. Still, I must believe Mother's and Father's characters are beyond reproach.

When I lie, it's because I'm terrified. I've learned a few things about their pasts. Mother healed sick people. Father tortured and executed the ones she healed—or at least that's what my aunt told me. But I need to believe that my da's character rises above my aunt's accusations.

Because if that Southern preacher was right about a father's sins haunting his kids, I am beyond screwed.

Period.

A student in the library carrel across from me shuffles her papers, drawing me back to Mother's journal. Mouth dry and hands shaking, I open it and dare to read the first page.

Mother's serene, alto voice seems to replace mine.

> Leo Tolstoy said, "I sit on a man's back, choking him, and making him carry me, and yet assure myself and others that I am very sorry for him and wish to ease his lot by any means possible, except getting off his back."

> I never wanted to be that person, riding on top of another's misery.

My name is Daniela Rose Cavanaugh.

Daddy called me the Orphan Dreamer. I called him *rafiki*, "my friend" in Swahili, the language of my ancestors.

Mom called me Daniela Rose Cavanaugh—on the rare occasions when she was mad at me— or Danny Rose for short. I'm her firstborn and her last. When I was a few minutes old, the doctor performed a hysterectomy on her, due to uncontrollable uterine bleeding. I learned about her surgery during one of our girl talks. In addition to calling her Mom, I also called her a kindred soul—a more endearing title than Mother.

My Irish grandmother escaped the Irish famine.

My Cherokee forefathers walked the Trail of Tears.

My African ancestors crossed the Atlantic Ocean, packed like sardines into a slaver's wooden tomb.

My Mongolian relations descended from Genghis Khan.

My English ancestors traveled on the Mayflower, escaping the yoke of the British Crown while seeking religious freedom in the New World. On July 4, 1776, they signed the Declaration of Independence and cast their chains off forever.

Compassion gives more generously than any inanimate religious title can, so I rarely call myself a Christian. I am a follower of Yeshua—the One who said, "For God so loved the whole world that He gave" and then spread His arms wide, sparing not even His life after saying, "Father, forgive them for they do not know what they do." He is the essence of compassion and life, so He lives, gently giving this invitation to those with an open heart: "Follow Me."

To ask an American of Cherokee, African, Mongolian, Irish, and English descent to separate her faith from her story would be as sacrilegious as asking a WWII Jewish veteran to fly a Nazi flag in his front yard.

Or must I scour the DNA, stories, and faith of my ancestors from my soul and story and hide them to please you? Neither can be done without killing my spirit. Is the purpose of political correctness to silence a viewpoint until we bleach the spice of life from the American spirit and resemble a track of nondescript suburban homes?

My questions will not matter tomorrow.

Some say knowledge of one's joyful ending can make the present misery tolerable. But who knows if one's last act will be full of joy or sorrow? Maybe we all sense our final act and don't realize it, or maybe we deny the facts of our final curtain call. Inspired by the One whose beginning and ending defies time—the Alpha and Omega—an ancient prophet wrote, "And as it is appointed unto men once to die, but after this the judgment." I am no prophet; I am a woman and a mother, but I am sure this saying applies to me as well.

Adelaide Rose, my love, if I had known my ending, how would I have lived my beginning?

—Daniela Rose Cavanaugh

Mother's voice trails off into oblivion, and I sniffle and dab my eyes. "You would have lived as you have—amazingly well, my kindred spirit."

Her thoughts invite me to a place of peaceful discovery, and I continue to read my parents' stories.

I will not judge.

I am their darling daughter, and according to my mother, I am breathtakingly beautiful, brave, and very sane. An Irishwoman's fiery-red hair spills down my back in tumbles of ringlets. Father gifted me his pale hue and winter blues, tinged with flecks of amber and green. African and

Sri Lankan blood courses through my veins, splashing my cheeks with cocoa-colored freckles.

A bat cave, sun-deprived version of Meghan Markle, the Duchess of Sussex, with red hair.

That's me.

Could Cordy Grey's memoir about my parents create a Simmie Knox portrait out of their legacies? Ten pages through the journal, I ache for Mom's embrace. Here is their story: an orphan, and the girl who dreams of him—the Orphan Dreamer and her glass tattoo. I share their secrets. They're about all I have left of my family—their memories, their stories hidden in the words of Mom's journals.

You judge.

Or don't.

But if my mother and my father had not lived, then I hope you'd be down with Pluto because Earth would've had different occupants, and because we would've needed a new home, that thimble-sized star sometimes known as a planet, a.k.a. Pluto, would've been our best option for a new address!

A voice seems to whisper, "Take me to the stars, oily boy . . ."

"Mummy, is that you?" I clench Mother's journal to my chest.

—THE END—

"We Wear the Mask" by Paul Laurence Dunbar

We wear the mask that grins and lies,
It hides our cheeks and shades our eyes,
This debt we pay to human guile;
With torn and bleeding hearts we smile,
And mouth with myriad subtleties

Why should the world be over-wise,
In counting all our tears and sighs?
Nay, let them only see us, while
    We wear the mask.

We smile, but, O great Christ, our cries
To thee from tortured souls arise.
We sing, but oh the clay is vile
Beneath our feet, and long the mile;
But let the world dream otherwise,
    We wear the mask!

Dear Reader,

Please continue the Orphan Dreamer Saga when you purchase and read the first novel-length book in the series, *Orphan Dreamer and the Glass Tattoo* (ODGT).

Also, *HouseGuest*, a prequel and a novelette, as well as *A Generation of Lighted Evergreens* (GLE), a prequel and a novelette, will be available soon. Thank you for joining Daniela and Cillian on the Orphan Dreamer's Journey. An excerpt of ODGT, *HouseGuest* and GLE can be found after the Author Biography page. Enjoy!

Happy Reading,
J. Nell Brown

Acknowledgments

Yeshua, thank you for inspiring this book through my imagination at a time when I needed it most. You've always been faithful to me.

Special thanks to my late father, Chaplain Austin Brown; my mother, Mrs. Jeanette Brown; and my sisters and friends.

To my editors, Ann Castro and Emily Dings at AnnCastro Studio, Faralee Pozo at Upwork.com, and Courtney Rae Andersson at Elevation Editorial—thank you all for your eagle-eye talents.

To my readers, thank you for loving this story. These characters exist for you.

Dear Reader,

Thoughtful book reviews about an author's work are like a pay raise or a tip to employees in traditional jobs. If you enjoyed this novelette, Orphan Dreamer and the Missing Arrowhead, please take a moment to place a review wherever you purchased this novelette, sharing with other readers what you've enjoyed. Your feedback is invaluable. Please ask your friends and family to purchase a copy of this novelette and read the series along with you. Book club questions will be available on my website, www.JNellBrown.com.

The A21 Campaign, a nonprofit organization to abolish the human trafficking of children, is my charity of choice. When you purchase a novelette or novel in the Orphan Dreamer saga, ten percent of the profits will be donated to A21 Campaign or organizations with a similar mission.

I look forward to saying hello to you on Facebook. Please like my page so you can keep up with my writing journey. Also, please sign up for my semiannual newsletter, and I will notify you about future releases, sales, and special events.

With gratitude,
J. Nell Brown

Author Biography

J. Nell Brown, the daughter of a chaplain and a teacher, is a Florida native.

Her relationship with Yeshua (Jesus) is fused with experiences in life, travel, extensive Bible study, and people's stories, and she combines all of this to create characters, plots, and settings for her novels and short stories. An involuntary insomniac, Brown practices medicine and writes in her free time.

She is a self-proclaimed nerd and loves all things scientific. Her love of science is demonstrated by her research at Los Alamos National Laboratory, the site for the development of the atomic bomb. She graduated with honors from the University of Florida (U of F) College of Agriculture and received her medical doctorate from the same.

After completing an anesthesia residency at The University of Chicago Hospitals, she began practicing in Florida.

Her heart overflows with compassion for people who are hurting, particularly children. A portion of the proceeds from this book will go to the A21 Campaign, a rescue charity for human-trafficked children, and Eastside Baptist School in Gainesville, Florida, a school of love, values, and solid educational curriculum for children whose parents would not otherwise be able to afford an alternative school education.

Her first nonfiction book, *Shhh, My Father Is Speaking, and I Am Listening,* is about her prayer journey. The Bible is her favorite literary masterpiece. You may follow J. Nell Brown on her author website, JNellBrown.com.

Orphan Dreamer and the Glass Tattoo

39—Adelaide: #Goodbye, Mom and Dad

The Present, the End . . .
03:49 A.M.
Friday, May 11
Exeter, New Hampshire

I SHOULD BE SLEEPING.

I want to, but I can't.

Rain falls, thrumming down the windowpanes of my dorm, smearing a haze across the night sky. I tug my great-great-grandmother's quilt up over my slight frame, blocking the night winds as they slap dead branches against the windows before seeping around rotting-wood casements and swirling around the room.

Cordy's asleep.

I'm jealous.

A ghoulish hand seems to slide through the night, clutching a sickle in its bloodless grasp. Its icy presence chills me to my bones.

Desperate to shake the creepy feeling I've had all day, I borrowed Gage's prayer candles. I light them. They flicker, casting shadows on bare walls but refusing to give me any comfort as they burn inside small red votives, leaving pools of wax in glass. Why do people burn candles in religious ceremonies anyway? I tighten my grip around Mother's letter. *My Dearest Adelaide Rose . . .*

She adored the Seurat painting, and now it belongs to me.

Where would I hang it? The dorms? Priceless paintings combined with chipped, pressboard furniture? Definitely bad Feng Shui.

Where would I live after Mother died?

The day before Da disappeared, he'd called me at 5:00 a.m. EST and confessed why he was acting weird —spontaneous.

"Yer mother's dying, lass. I dinnae ken how else to say it to you."

"Can we help her?" I asked.

"I cannae save her. Her doctor says it's too late fer a lung transplant." My da's voice sounded as though it would break, not a frequent occurrence. His physical presence usually barked, "Think twice before acting stupid."

"What is she dying from?"

"Blood's floodin' her lungs, and she's drownin'. Fate's cruel. She's always hated water—lakes, oceans, pools—it didna matter. Never mastered swimmin'. Now her heart's broken, and I'm tellin' the good Lord, I didna break it. I'm a man of blood. I've never deserved her."

I'm a man of blood. I never deserved her.

My heart skips a beat, then pounds my ribs.

I tuck Mother's note inside my flannel pajamas, placing it close to my heart as I thought about Da's phone call. "Mummy, get better. Stay a while longer, please?" I breathe the plea into the darkness, but my voice won't travel the hundreds of miles from New Hampshire to the Blue Ridge Mountains of North Carolina where she lives alone with Beatha, her friend and, according to Father, her nurse.

It sucks to be a teenager.

Adults keep us in the dark and then wonder why we bump into things.

I need clarity. I've never done this before—closed my eyes, knelt, and prayed. "A month longer with Mummy. That's all I ask. Let her watch me graduate."

I open my eyes, already knowing that today is going to be a sucky, armpit kind of day. Since leaving the library and going to bed, I've been staring at the ceiling for six hours.

Red block numbers on the face of my digital clock tell me it is 3:49 in the morning.

Before the sun dares to rise, I slip on a pair of spandex leggings, a lavender hoodie, well-worn trainers, and my shoulder lamp, then stuff my mother's letter into the hoodie pocket. I need to be near her. The letter is all I have.

Tiptoeing from my dorm room, I'm careful to not wake Cordelia.

I need to be alone.

Beneath an audience of stars, I jog across the slick, wet grounds of Exeter Academy. Cold sweat drips down my back. Endorphins flood my muscles, and I pump my arms and legs harder, charging past my lecture hall, a redbrick, four-story building hidden behind a cluster of maple trees. Fog hovers over the lawn, and crickets whistle a nightingale's song.

Out of nowhere, a wobbly form charges toward me.

My heart races, fueling my legs.

The creature's stride quickens, and as it comes closer, I recognize him. He's uglier in the dark, like a swamp monster on two legs.

HouseGuest

1

IMMORTALS—TIME WITHOUT END

I'M IN A COLD CAVE, which is rather ironic because I'm in hell.

Tsk. Tsk. Don't pity me. After the moon drips with blood, I will come for you. Until then, I'm here at my summer residence, prepping for our meeting—Armageddon, the day I scrub Earth clean of its invaders.

You.

My most treasured possession sits beside me while humans squint, then peek through the optics of a telescope only to ask, "Is there an intelligent life form in outer space?" I laugh. Only a nitwit and self-centered creature would look into a telescope and ask such a stupid question. If a creature requires a telescope to see me, they are working at a disadvantage.

I see you.

Here's looking at you, kid. No optics. No lens. No convex shiny mirrors. No telescope. And now it's my turn to ask, "Does any intelligent life exist on Earth?"

I already know the answer: No, not yet. But very soon. I look down past Earth's atmosphere. The moon is full. Bright. White. One day it will darken to blood red at the right time. Then, we will come back, and there will only be enough room for one species—mine.

"Welcome home, Nomed," I say to myself, eager for the day when Aglaope whispers these three words into my ear as we stand side by side on the sugary-white beaches of Key West, Florida, or the snow-packed ridges of Mount Everest. I love the cold. It suits me.

"You're in good practice." Aglaope smiles at me.

"I'm ready. No. *We're* ready to return home, Agla." I gaze into the distance. Cloaked in secrecy, my winter home approaches Earth. Ah, when a plan comes together!

We call our Trojan horse Wormwood. Larger than the sun, the invisible planet hides in the shadows of Earth's universe, deep in a wormhole that no human has dared to explore. Besides, the inky black entrance into that wormhole appears as a tiny speck through Earth's most powerful telescopes. My warriors train day and night in preparation for our day of reckoning—the day we invade Earth and take it back, making the planet great once again.

"When they see Wormwood, it will be too late, Agla."

"And that's why you're his general, Nomed. Cunning. Ruthless. Decisive." Her left eye scarred shut, Aglaope gazes into my left eye. "Could a human fight your warriors and win?"

"Of course."

"But you promised me!" She pulls away from my embrace. "You promised that all would be well. That I would be safe."

"They could win if they knew how to fight us. But they don't know how to fight us, and their bullets, nuclear warheads, aircraft carriers, and submarines will be useless in this fight. They will kill themselves. But not us. Never fear. Humans couldn't figure out how to give life if they tried. How long have they played around in the most prestigious laboratories, yet not cured cancer?"

"This weapon . . ." Aglaope reaches for my hand. "What is it?"

"I hold this secret closer to my bosom than I have held you."

"Nomed, tell me," she whines.

"No! It's for your protection, my love. Do not ask me again."

A Generation of Lighted Evergreens

I—Sugarcane

12:00 P.M.
Friday, August 11, 1967
Belle Glade, Florida

AUSTIN CAVANAUGH HAD BEEN IN the same position for the last five hours—slightly hunched with a machete in his right hand, chopping sugarcane in a hot, humid field.

He laid the cutlass by his feet, dug in his pocket, and retrieved a gray-brown handkerchief, a Christmas gift from his father, who had been a peanut farmer. Dabbing his forehead, he soaked up droplets of sweat, a field hand's reminder that the old fireball didn't play favorites. "Whaddya say, 'bout time for some water, Chuck?"

"When the boss man says so." Chuck kept chopping

down stalks of cane. He was Austin's local friend and had grown up in Gainesville, Florida, down the dirt road from Austin's father's peanut farm.

"Ain't no rest for the weary . . ." Austin's arm ached as he gripped the wooden handle of his machete, swiping the blade through another clump of thick cane.

"You ain't takin' a break without the whistle chirpin', are ya?" Riddled with the remnants of untreated pneumonia and asthma, Chuck hacked up strands of mustard-colored phlegm. The dirt and pollen hadn't helped his allergies or lung infection.

"Nope—just dreamin'."

"What about?"

"A cozy place in the country, a vegetable garden, a few chickens, a hammock, and a tall glass of ice-cold lemonade." Austin kneaded his wrist, easing the constant throb. "How's the pneumonia?"

"I ain't laid out yet. You'll know it's bad when I fall over dead."

"Don't want it to come to that. Will the doc see you?"

"He ain't never seen no colored people."

"But he takes care of sick people, don't he?"

"Yep."

"You're sick."

"You done died and gone to heaven. Yes, sirree." Chuck rocked back on his heels, his thumbs tucked beneath his blue suspenders. "You lost your mind somewhere in this cane field." As though stepping on a drumline, Chuck dipped to the right. "Go on wit yo bad self."

Austin gazed into the heavens. Closing his eyes, he allowed Florida's sun to bake his skin to a deeper brown.

No need to keep the sun from doing her business. Brown was brown in the South. It didn't matter if you had one teaspoon of cream in your DNA or ten, so be proud of the Almighty's doing.

"Whatcha doin'?"

"Thinkin'."

"Oh, Lord . . ." Chuck's gaze skimmed over the cane field.

A channel of wind found its way between the stalks. Leaves slipped by each other, creating a fan.

Opening his eyes, Austin turned and stared down the wide dirt road that wound like a diamondback rattlesnake. The dirt and pebble path ended at the big house—a white, rectangular clapboard building adorned with black shutters and six twelve-pane windows. A deep wraparound porch encircled the boss's field house like his belt—low and dipping in the front. Austin knew about the belt because the boss had chased him down the road, threatening to use it.

The reason?

Austin's yellow lab, Gus, hadn't stayed put—the boss had found him down the main road, tucked beneath a shrub. Old Gus had probably spotted the shady boughs of the sugarcane field's lone oak tree and decided he needed a little more cool air, or he had mindlessly chased a squirrel, which gave him an excuse to track his master's scent. The reason hadn't mattered, and since then, Austin had shut Gus inside their wooden shack by the stream.

Hope he's not gone and fainted in that old shed. Couldn't bear to find him laid out from the heat.

Hunching low, Chuck tiptoed to Austin's side, breaking his thoughts. When Chuck grinned, a space the size of a man's thumb separated his dingy teeth—teeth like a black-top wedged between two dirty-white fishtail Cadillacs. A drunken brawl in the juke joint had claimed his missing teeth, but who was Austin to judge a man's past? He swept his machete across the bases of several stalks of cane, excising them with an executioner's accuracy.

One paycheck closer to a better life.

www.ingramcontent.com/pod-product-compliance
Lightning Source LLC
Chambersburg PA
CBHW030649190726
48286CB00008B/2725